There's a Monster in my Bed!

BY SUE INMAN
ILLUSTRATED BY ERIC KINCAID

BRIMAX • NEWMARKET • ENGLAND

"I'm tired," said Mother Bear to Father Bear.
"I need a good, long sleep."

While Father Bear was cleaning his teeth, Mother Bear went into the nursery to check on the baby bears. She kissed Big Baby Bear. She kissed Little Baby Bear. She kissed Tiny Baby Bear. "Goodnight, Baby Bears. Sleep tight!" said Mother Bear.

Then Mother Bear and Father Bear snuggled up together in their warm bed. They were just dropping off to sleep when Mother Bear heard the sound of little paws padding into the room.

She opened a sleepy eye and saw Big Baby Bear.
"There's a monster in my bed," said Big Baby Bear.
"There are no such things as monsters," mumbled
Mother Bear. "Go back to sleep."
"But I'm frightened," said Big Baby Bear. "Please let
me get in with you."
"Oh, all right then," said Mother Bear.

So Father Bear moved over and Mother Bear moved over, and Big Baby Bear climbed in beside her.

"Goodnight," they all said to each other. Then they went back to sleep. After a while, Mother Bear heard Little Baby Bear padding into the room.

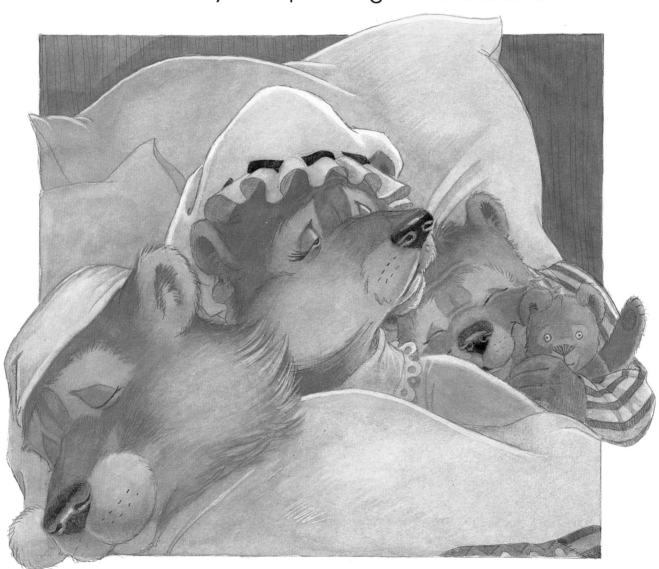

"There's a monster in my bed," said Little Baby Bear.

"No there isn't," growled Mother Bear. "Go back to sleep."

"But I'm frightened," said Little Baby Bear. "Please let me get in with you."

"Oh, all right. Anything for some peace and quiet," said Mother Bear.

So Father Bear moved over and Mother Bear moved over and Big Baby Bear moved over, and Little Baby Bear climbed into bed.

"Goodnight," they all said to each other, and they settled down to sleep.

Just as Mother Bear was dropping off to sleep again, she heard Tiny Baby Bear padding into the room.

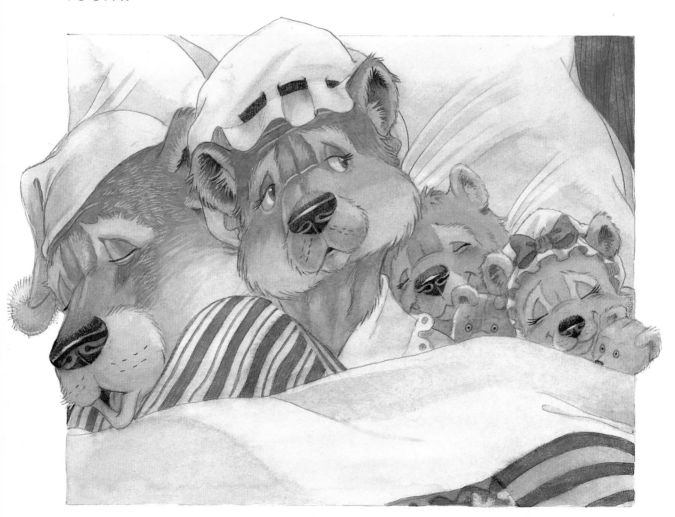

"There's a monster in my bed," said Tiny Baby Bear.
"NO THERE ISN'T!" snarled Mother Bear.
"But I'm frightened," said Tiny Baby Bear. "Please let me get in with you."
"Oh, all right," said Mother Bear with a sigh.

So Father Bear moved over and Mother Bear moved over and Big Baby Bear moved over and Little Baby Bear moved over, and Tiny Baby Bear climbed in.

"Goodnight," they all said to each other. Then they settled back down to sleep.

They had not been asleep for very long when Tiny
Baby Bear wriggled. Then Little Baby Bear jiggled.
And Big Baby Bear wiggled. Then Mother Bear
rolled over, and Father Bear fell out of bed.

"Humph!" said Father Bear. "I was too squashed in that bed anyway." So he picked up his teddy and went to sleep in the baby bears' bed.

The baby bears' bed was soft and warm, and there was plenty of room for Father Bear to spread out. Soon he was fast asleep and snoring happily.

Back in the big bed, all was peaceful for a while. But then Tiny Baby Bear wriggled. Then Little Baby Bear jiggled. And Big Baby Bear rolled over. And Mother Bear fell out of bed.

"Humph!" said Mother Bear. "I was too squashed in that bed anyway." So she got up and climbed into the baby bears' bed. Mother Bear settled down next to Father Bear. She felt warm and sleepy. Soon she was snoring, too.

When morning came, Father Bear woke up.
He stretched and yawned and blinked his eyes.
Then he blinked again. For there, lying in the bed
next to him, was something *horrible*. It was big and
brown and hairy and it was making a most
peculiar noise.
"Aaaaaagh!" said Father Bear. "There's a monster
in the bed!"

The noise woke the horrible, big, brown, hairy thing.
It sat up sleepily.
"Where's a monster?" it said...
In Mother Bear's voice.

ISBN 1 85854 574 9
Published by Brimax Books Ltd, Newmarket, England, CB8 7AU, 1997.
Printed in France - n° 70135 - A